GULITH

Castaways Of Eros

Nelson S. Bond

ISBN: 978-1-63652-313-2

CASTAWAYS OF EROS

NELSON S. BOND

TABLE OF CONTENTS

I

B obby couldn't help wishing Pop would stand up just a little bit straighter. Not that he was ashamed of Pop; it wasn't that at all. It was just that the Patrolman stood *so* straight, his shoulders broad and firm. Standing beside him made Pop look sort of thin and puny; his chest caved in like he was carrying a heavy weight on his shoulders.

That was from studying things through a microscope. Anyhow, decided Bobby with a fierce loyalty, that S.S.P. man probably wouldn't even know what to look for if somebody put a microscope in front of him. Even if he was big and sturdy and broad-shouldered in his space blues.

Mom said, "Bobby, what *are* you muttering about? Do stop fidgeting!" Bobby said, "Yessum," and glared at Moira, as if she, in some obscure way, were to blame for his having been reprimanded right out here in the middle of Long Island Spaceport, where everybody could hear and laugh at him. But Moira, studying the handsome S.S.P. man surreptitiously, did not notice. Dick was fixing something in the ship. Eleanor stood quietly beside Mom, crooning softly to The Pooch so it wouldn't be scared by the thunderous blast of rocket motors. Grampaw Moseley had button-holed an embarrassed young ensign, was complaining to him in loud and certain terms that modern astronavigation practices were, "Rank bellywash, Mister, and a dad-ratted disgrace!"

The Patrolman said, "Your name, please, Sir?"

"Robert Emmet O'Brien Moseley," said Pop.

"Occupation?"

"Research physicist, formerly. Now about to become a land-grant settler."

"Age of self and party ... former residence...."

Overhead, the sky was blue and thin—clear as a bowl of skimmed milk; its vastness limned in sharp relief, to the west and north, the mighty spans and arches, the faery domes and flying buttresses of Great New York. The spacedrome fed a hundred ducts of flight; from one field lifted air locals, giddy, colored motes with gyroscopes aspin. From another, a West Coast stratoliner surged upward to lose itself in thin, dim heights.

Vast cradles by the Sound were the nests to which a flock of interplanetary craft made homeward flight. Luggers and barges and cruisers. Bobby saw, with sudden excitement, the sharp, starred prow of the Solar Space Patrol man-o'-war.

Here, in this field, the GSC's—the General Spacecraft Cradles. From one of which, as soon as Pop got clearance, their ship would take off. Their ship! Bobby felt an eager quickening of his pulse; his stomach was aswarm with a host of butterflies. *Their ship!*

The space officer said, "I think that takes care of everything, Dr. Moseley. I presume you understand the land-grant laws and obligations?"

"Yes, Lieutenant."

"Very well, then—" Space-red hands made official motions with a hand-stamp and pen. "Your clearance. And my very best wishes, Sir."

"Thank you," said Pop quietly. He turned. "That's all. Ready, Mother? Eleanor? Moira?"

Bobby bounded forward. "Can I push the button, can I, Pop? When we start, can I?"

Dick was waiting before the open lock of the *Cuchulainn*. Dick could do anything, everything at once. He took The Pooch into the circle of his left arm, helped his mother aboard, said, "Shut up, kid, you're enough to wake the dead. Watch that guard-panel, Elly. Papers all set, Pop?" And he tickled The Pooch's dimpled cheek with an oily finger. "You act just like your mama," he said irrelevantly, and the baby gurgled. Eleanor cried, "Dick—those dirty hands!"

"Everything is in order, Richard," said Pop.

"Good. You folks go in and strap down. I'll seal. Here comes the cradle-monkey now."

Pop said, "Come along, Robert," and the others went inside. Bobby waited, though, to see the cradle-monkey, the man under whose orders spacecraft lifted gravs. The cradle-monkey was a dour man with gnarled legs and arms and temper. He looked at the *Cuchulainn* and sniffed; then at Dick.

"Family crate, huh?"

"That's right."

"Well, f'r goddlemighty' sakes, don't try to blast off with y'r side jets burnin'. Take a seven-point-nineteen readin' on y'r Akka gauge, stern rockets only—"

"Comets to you, butt-hoister!" grinned Dick. "I've had eight years on the spider run. I can lift this can."

"Oh, a rocketeer?" There was new, grudging respect in the groundman's tone. "Well, how was I t' know? Y'ought t' see what some o' them jaloupi-jockeys do to my cradles—burn 'em black! Oh, well—" He backed away from the ship.

"Clean ether!" said Dick. He closed the lock. Its seal-brace slid into place, wheezing asthmatically. Bobby's ears rang suddenly with the mild compression of air; when he swallowed, they were all right again. Dick saw him. "What are you doing here, kid? Didn't I hear Pop tell you to come below?"

Bobby said, "I'm not a kid. I'm almost sixteen."

"Just old enough," promised Dick, "to get your seat warmed if you don't do what you're told. Remember, you're a sailor on a spaceship now. Pop's the Skipper, and I'm First Mate. If you don't obey orders, it's mutiny, and—"

"I'm obeying," said Bobby hastily. He followed his brother down the corridor, up the ramp, to the bridge. "Can I push the button when we take off, huh, Dick?"

After his high expectations, it wasn't such a great thrill. Dick set the stops and dials, told him which button to press. "When I give the word, kid." Of course, he got to sit in the pilot's bucket-chair, which was something. Moira and Eleanor and Mom to lie down in acceleration hammocks while Pop and Dick sat in observation seats. He waited, all ears and nerves, as the slow seconds sloughed away. Pop set the hypos running; their faint, dull throb was a magic sound in the silence.

Then there came a signal from outside. Dick's hand rose in understanding response; fell again. "Now!"

Bobby jabbed the button in frantic haste. Suddenly the silence was shattered by a thunderous detonation. There was a massive hand pressing him back into the soft, yielding leather of his chair; the chair retreated on oiled channels, pneumatic compensators hissing faintly, absorbing the shock. Across the room a faulty hammock-hinge squeaked rustily.

Then it was over as quickly as it had begun, and he could breathe again, and Dick was lurching across the turret on feet that wobbled queerly because up was down and top was bottom and everything was funny and mixed up.

Dick cut in the artificial gravs, checked the meter dials with a hurried glance, smiled.

"Dead on it! Want to check, Skipper?"

But Pop was standing by the observation pane, eyeing an Earth already ball-like in the vastness of space. Earth, dwindling with each passing moment. Bobby moved to his side and watched; Moira, too, and Eleanor and Mom, and even Dick.

Pop touched Mom's hand. He said, "Martha—I'm not sure this is fair to you and the children. Perhaps it isn't right that I should force my dream on all of you. The world we have known and loved lies behind us. Before us lies only uncertainty...."

Mom sort of sniffed and reached for a handkerchief. She turned her back to Pop for a minute, and when she turned around again her eyes were red and angry-looking. She said, "*You* want to go on, don't you, Rob?"

Pop nodded. "But I'm thinking of you, Martha."

"Of me!" Mom snorted indignantly. "Hear him talk! I never heard such nonsense in my life. Of *course* I want to go on. No, never mind that! Richard, isn't there a kitchen on this boat?"

"A galley, Mom. Below."

"Galley ... kitchen ... what's the difference? You two girls come with me. I'll warrant these men are starving. *I* am!"

After that, things became so normal as to be almost disappointing. From his eager reading of such magazines as *Martian Tales* and *Cosmic Fiction Weekly*, Bobby had conceived void-travel to be one long, momentous chain of adventure. A super-thrilling serial, punctuated by interludes with space-pirates, narrow brushes with meteors, sabotage, treachery—hair-raising, heroic and horrifying.

There was nothing like that to disturb the calm and peaceful journey of the *Cuchulainn*. Oh, it was enjoyable to stare through the observation panes at the flame-dotted pall of space—until Pop tried to turn his curious interest into educational channels; it was exciting, too, to probe through the corridored recesses of their floating home—except that Dick issued strict orders that nothing must be touched, that he must not enter certain chambers, that he mustn't push his nose into things that didn't concern kids—

Which offended Bobby, who was sixteen, or, anyway, fifteen and three-quarters.

So they ate and they slept and they ate again. And Pop and Dick spelled each other at the control banks. Moira spent endless hours with comb and mirror, devising elaborate hair-dos which—Bobby reminded her with impudent shrewdness—were so much wasted energy, since they were settling in a place where nobody could see them. And Mom bustled about in the galley, performing miracles with flour and stuff, and in the recreation room, Eleanor minded The Pooch, and lost innumerable games of cribbage to Grampaw Moseley who cheated outrageously and groused, between hands, about the dad-blame nonsensical way Dick was handling the ship.

And somehow three Earth days sped by, and they were nearing their destination. The tiny planetoid, Eros.

Pop said, "You deserve a great deal of credit, son, for your fine work in rehabilitating the *Cuchulainn*. It has performed beautifully. You are a good spaceman."

Dick flushed. "She's a good ship, Pop, even if she is thirty years old. Some of these old, hand-fashioned jobs are better than the flash junk they're turning off the belts nowadays. You've checked the declension and trajectory?"

"Yes. We should come within landing radius in just a few hours. Cut drives at 19.04.22 precisely and make such minor course alterations as are necessary, set brakes." Pop smiled happily. "We're very fortunate, son. A mere fifteen million miles. It's not often Eros is so near Earth."

"Don't I know it? It's almost a hundred million at perihelion. But that's not the lucky part. You sure had to pull strings to get the government land grant to Eros. What a plum! Atmosphere ... water ... vegetable life ... all on a hunk of dirt fifty-seven miles in diameter. Frankly, I don't get it! Eros must have terrific mass to have the attributes of a full-sized planet."

"It does, Richard. A neutronium core."

"Neutronium!" Dick gasped. "Why don't people tell me these things? Roaring craters, Pop, we're rich! Bloated plutocrats!"

"Not so fast, son. Eventually, perhaps; not today. First we must establish our claims, justify our right to own Eros. That means work, plenty of hard work. After that, we might be able to consider a mining operation. What's that?"

Bobby jumped. It was Mom's voice. But her cry was not one of fear, it was one of excitement.

"Rob, look! Off to the—the left, or the port, or whatever you call it! Is that our new home?"

Bobby did not need to hear Pop's reply to know that it was. His swift intake of breath was enough, the shine in his eyes as he peered out the observation port.

"Eros!" he said.

It looked all right to Bobby. A nice, clean little sphere, spinning lazily before their eyes like a top someone had set in motion, then gone away and forgotten. Silver and green and rusty brown, all still faintly blued by distance. The warm rays of old Sol reflected gaily, giddily, from seas that covered half the planetoid's surface, and mountains cut long, jagged shadows into sheltered plains beneath them. It was, thought Bobby, not a bad looking little place. But not anything to get all dewy-eyed about, like Pop was.

Dick said softly, "All right, Pop. Let's check and get ready to set 'er down...."

II

I t was not Dick's fault. It was just a tough break that no one had expected, planned for, guarded against. The planetoid was there beneath them; they would land on it. It was as simple at that.

Only it wasn't. Nor did they have any warning that the problem was more complex until it was too late to change their plans, too late to halt the irrevocable movements of a grounding spaceship. Dick should have known, of course. He was a spaceman; he had served two tricks on the Earth-Venus-Mars run. But all those planets were large; Eros was just a mote. A spinning top....

Anyway, it was after the final coordinates had been plotted, the last bank control unchangeably set, the rockets cut, that they saw the curved knife-edge of black slicing up over Eros' rim. For a long moment Dick stared at it, a look of angry chagrin in his eyes.

"Well, blast me for an Earth-lubbing idiot! Do you see that, Pop?"

Pop looked like he had shared Dick's persimmon.

"The night-line. We forgot to consider the diurnal revolution."

"And now we've got to land in the dark. On strange terrain. Arragh! I should have my head examined. I've got a plugged tube somewhere!"

Grampaw Moseley hobbled in, appraised the situation with his incomparable ability to detect something amiss. He snorted and rattled his cane on the floor.

"They's absolutely nothin'," he informed the walls, "to this hereditation stuff. Elst why should my own son an' his son be so dag-nabbed stoopid?"

"'What can't be cured,'" said Pop mildly, "'must be endured.' We have the forward search-beams, son. They will help."

That was sheer optimism. As they neared the planet its gravitational attraction seized them tighter and tighter until they were completely under its compulsion. Dusk swept down upon them, the sunlight dulled, faded, grayed. Then as the ship nosed downward, suddenly all was black. The yellow beam of the search stabbed reluctant shadows, bringing rocky crags and rounded tors into swift, terrifying relief.

Dick snapped, "Into your hammocks, everyone! Don't worry. This crate will stand a lot of bust-up. It's tough. A little bit of luck—"

But there was perspiration on his forehead, and his fingers played over the control banks like frightened moths.

There was no further need for the artificial gravs. Eros exerted, strangely, incredibly, an attractive power almost as potent as Earth's. Dick cut off the gravs, then the hypos. As the last machine-created sound died away from the cabin, Bobby heard the high scream of atmosphere, raging and tearing at the *Cuchulainn* with angry fingers.

Through howling Bedlam they tumbled dizzily and for moments that were ages long. While Dick labored frantically at the controls, while Moira watched with bated breath. Mom said nothing, but her hand sought Pop's; Eleanor cradled The Pooch closer to her. Grampaw scowled.

And then, suddenly—

"Hold tight! We're grounding!" cried Dick.

And instinctively Bobby braced himself for a shock. But there was only a shuddering jar, a lessening of the roar that beat upon their eardrums, a dull, flat thud. A sodden, heavy grinding and the groan of metal forward. Then a false nausea momentarily assailed him. Because for the first time in days the *Cuchulainn* was completely motionless.

Dick grinned shakily. "Well!" he said. "Well!"

Pop unbuckled his safety belt, climbed gingerly out of his hammock, moved to the port, slid back its lock-plate. Bobby said, "Can you see anything, Pop? Can you?" And Mom, who could read Pop's expressions like a book, said, "What is it, Rob?"

Pop stroked his chin. He said, "Well, we've landed safely, Richard. But I'm afraid we've—er—selected a wet landing field. We seem to be under water!"

His hazard was verified immediately. Indisputably. For from the crack beneath the door leading from the control turret to the prow-chambers of the ship, came a dark trickle that spread and puddled and stained and gurgled. Water!

Dick cried, "Hey, this is bad! We'd better get out of here—"

He leaped to his controls. Once more the plaintive hum of the hypatomics droned through the cabin, gears ground and clashed as the motors caught, something forward exploded dully, distantly. The ship rocked and trembled, but did not move. Again Dick tried to jet the fore-rockets. Again, and yet again.

And on the fourth essay, there ran through the ship a violent shudder, broken metal grated shrilly from forward, and the water began bubbling and churning through the crack. Deeper and swifter. Dick cut motors and turned, his face an angry mask.

"We can't get loose. The entire nose must be stove in! We're leaking like a sieve. Look, everybody—get into your bulgers. We'll get out through the airlock!"

Mom cried, "But—but our supplies, Dick! What are we going to do for food, clothing, furniture—?"

"We'll worry about that later. Right now we've got to think of ourselves. That-aboy, Bobby! Thanks for getting 'em out. You girls remember how to climb into 'em? Eleanor—you take that oversized one. That's right. There's room for you and The Pooch—"

The water was almost ankle deep in the control room by the time they had all donned spacesuits. Bloated figures in fabricoid bulgers, they followed Dick to the airlock. It was weird, and a little bit frightening, but to Bobby it was thrilling, too. This was the sort of thing you read stories about. Escape from a flooding ship....

They had time—or took time—to gather together a few precious belongings. Eleanor packed a carrier with baby food for The Pooch, Mom a bundle of provisions hastily swept from the galley bins; Pop remembered the medical kit and the tool-box, Grampaw was laden down with blankets and clothing, Dick burdened himself and Bobby with armloads of such things as he saw and forevisioned need for.

At the lock, Dick issued final instructions.

"The air in the bulgers will carry you right to the surface. We'll gather there, count noses, and decide on our next move. Pop, you go first to lead the way, then Mom, and Eleanor, Grampaw—"

Thus, from the heart of the doomed *Cuchulainn*, they fled. The airlock was small. There was room for but one at a time. The water was waist—no, breast-deep—by the time all were gone save Bobby and Dick. Bobby, whose imagination had already assigned him the command of the foundering ship, wanted to uphold the ancient traditions by being the last to leave. But Dick had other ideas. He shoved Bobby—not too gently—into the lock. Then there was water, black, solid, forbidding, about him. And the outer door opening.

He stepped forward. And floated upward, feeling an uneasy, quibbly feeling in his stomach. Almost immediately a hard something *clanged!* against his impervite helmet; it was a lead-soled bulger boot; then he was bobbing and tossing on shallow black wavelets beside the others.

Above him was a blue-black, star-gemmed sky; off to his right, not distant, was a rising smudge that must be the mainland. A dark blob popped out of the water. Dick.

Moira reached for the twisted branch.

Dick's voice was metallic through the audios of the space-helmet. "All here, Pop? Everybody all right? Swell! Let's strike out for the shore, there. Stick together, now. It isn't far."

Pop said, "The ship, Richard?"

"We'll find it again. I floated up a marking buoy. That round thing over there isn't Grampaw."

Grampaw's voice was raucous, belligerent. "You bet y'r boots it ain't! I'm on my way to terry firmy. The last one ashore's a sissy!"

Swimming in a bulger, Bobby found, was silly. Like paddling a big, warm, safe rubber rowboat. The stars winked at him, the soft waves explored his face-plate with curious, white fingers of spray. Pretty soon there was sand scraping his boots ... a long, smooth beach with rolling hills beyond.

In the sudden scarlet of dawn, it was impossible to believe the night had even been frightening. Throughout the night, the Moseley clan huddled together there on the beach, waiting, silent, wondering. But when the sun burst over the horizon like a clamoring, brazen gong, they looked upon this land which was their new home—and found it good.

The night did not last long. But Pop had told them it would not.

"Eros rotates on its axis," he explained, "in about ten hours, forty minutes, Earth time measurement. Therefore we shall have 'days' and 'nights' of five hours; short dawns or twilights. This will vary somewhat, you understand, with the change of seasons."

Dick asked, "Isn't that a remarkably slow rotation? For such a tiny planet, I mean? After all, Eros is only one hundred and eighty odd miles in circumference—"

"Eros has many peculiarities. Some of them we have discussed before. It approaches Earth nearer than any other celestial body, excepting Luna and an occasional meteor or comet. When first discovered by Witt, in 1898, the world of science marveled at finding a true planetoid with such an uncommon orbit. At perihelion it comes far within the orbit of Mars; at aphelion it is far outside.

"During its near approach in 1900-01, Eros was seen to vary in brightness at intervals of five hours and fifteen or twenty minutes. At that time, a few of the more imaginative astronomers offered the suggestion that this variation might be caused by diurnal rotation. After 1931, though, the planetoid fled from Earth. It was not until 1975, the period of its next approach, that the Ronaldson-Chenwith expedition visited it and determined the old presumption to be correct."

"We're not the first men to visit Eros, then?"

"Not at all. It was investigated early in the days of spaceflight. Two research foundations, the Royal Cosmographic Society and the Interplanetary Service, sent expeditions here. During the Black Douglass period of terrorism, the S.S.P. set up a brief military occupation. The Galactic Metals Corporation at one time attempted to establish mining operations here, but the Bureau refused them permission, for under the Spacecode of '08, it was agreed by the Triune that all asteroids should be settled under land-grant law.

"That is why," concluded Pop, "we are here now. As long as I can remember, it has been my dream to take a land-grant colony for my very own. Long years ago I decided that Eros should be my settlement. As you have said, Richard, it necessitated the pulling of many strings. Eros is a wealthy little planet; the man who earns it wins a rich prize. More than that, though—" Pop lifted his face to the skies, now blue with hazy morning. There was something terribly bright and proud in his eyes. "More than that, there is the desire to carve a home out of the wilderness. To be able to one day say, 'Here is my home that I have molded into beauty with my own hands.' Do you know what I mean, son? In this workaday world of ours there are no more Earthly frontiers for us to dare, as did our forefathers. But still within us all stirs the deep, instinctive longing to hew a new home from virgin land—"

His words dwindled into silence, and, inexplicably, Bobby felt awed. It was Grampaw Moseley who burst the queer moment into a thousand spluttering fragments.

"Talkin' about hewin'," he said, "S'posen we 'hew us a few vittles? Hey?"

Dick roused himself.

"Right you are, Grampaw," he said. "You can remove your bulgars. I've tested the air; it's fine and warm, just as the report said. Moira, while Mom and Eleanor are fixing breakfast, suppose you lay out our blankets and spare clothing to dry? Grampaw, get a fire going. Pop and Bobby and I will get some wood."

Thus Eros greeted its new masters, and the Moseleys faced morning in their new Eden.

III

————

Grampaw Moseley wiped his mouth with the back of his hand. There were no napkins, which suited him fine.

"It warn't," he said, "a bad meal. But it warn't a fust-class un, neither. Them synthos an' concentrates ain't got no more flavor than—"

Bobby agreed with him. Syntho ham wasn't too bad. It had a nice, meaty taste. And syntho coffee tasted pretty much like the real thing. But those syntho eggs tasted like nothing under the sun except just plain, awful syntho eggs.

Four Eros days—the equivalent of forty-two Earth hours or so—had passed since their crash landing. In that short time, much had been done to make their beach camp-site comfortable. All members of the family were waiting now for Dick to return.

Pop said seriously, "I'm afraid you'll have to eat them and like them for a little while, Father. We can't get fresh foods until we're settled; we can't settle until—Ah! Here comes Dick!"

"I'll eat 'em," grumbled Grampaw, "but be durned if I'll like 'em. What'd you l'arn, Dicky-boy?"

Dick removed his helmet, unzipped himself from his bulger, shook his head.

"It looks worse every time I go back. I may not be able to get in the airlock again if the ship keeps on settling. The whole prow split wide open when we hit, the ship is full of water. The flour and sugar and things like that are ruined. I managed to get a few more things out, though. Some tools, guns, wire—stuff like that."

"How about the hypatomic?"

"Let him eat, Rob," said Mom. "He's hungry."

"I can eat and talk at the same time, Mom. I think I can get the hypatomic out. I'd better, anyhow. If we're ever going to raise the ship, we'll need power. And atomic power is the only kind we can get in this wilderness." And he shook his head. "But we can't do it in a day or a week. It will take time."

"Time," said Pop easily, "is the one commodity with which we are over-supplied." He thought for a minute. "If that's the way it is, we might as well move."

"Move?" demanded Grampaw. "What's the matter with the place we're at?"

"For one thing, it's too exposed. An open beach is no place for a permanent habitation. So far we've been very lucky. We've had no storms. But for a permanent camp-site, we must select a spot further inland. A fertile place, where we can start crops. A place with fresh, running water, natural shelter against cold and wind and rain—"

"What'll we do?" grinned Dick. "Flip a coin?"

"No. Happily, there is a spot like that within an easy walk of here. I discovered it yesterday while studying the terrain." Pop took a stick, scratched a rude drawing on the sand before him. "This is the coastline. We landed on the west coast of this inlet. The land we see across there, that low, flat land, I judge to be delta islands. Due south of us is a fine, fresh-water river, watering fertile valleys to either side. There, I think, we should build."

Dick nodded.

"Fish from the sea, vegetables from our own farm—is there any game, Pop?"

"That I don't know. We haven't seen any. Yet."

"We'll find out. Will this place you speak of be close enough to let me continue working on the *Cuchulainn*? Yes? Well, that's that. When do we start?"

"Why not now? There's nothing to keep us here."

They packed their meager belongings while Dick finished his meal; the sun was high when they left the beach. They followed the shore line southward, the ground rising steadily before them. And before evening, they came to a rolling vale through which a sparkling river meandered lazily to the sea.

Small wonders unfolded before their eyes. Marching along, they had discovered that there was game on Eros. Not quite Earthly, of course—but that was not to be expected. There was one small, furry beast about the size of a rabbit, only its color was vivid leaf-green. Once, as they passed a wooded glen, a pale, fawnlike creature stole from the glade, watched them with soft, curious eyes. Another time they all started violently as the familiar siren of a Patrol monitor screamed raucously from above them; they looked up to see an irate, orange and jade-green bird glaring down at them.

And of course there were insects—

"There would have to be insects," Pop said. "There could be no fruitful vegetable life without insects. Plants need bees and crawling ants—or their equivalent—to carry the pollen from one flower to another."

They chose a site on the riverside, a half mile or so from, above, and overlooking the sea. They selected it because a spring of pure, bubbling water was nearby, because the woodlands dwindled away into lush fields. And Pop said,

"This is it. We'll build our home on yonder knoll. And who knows—" Again there grew that strange look in his eyes. "Who knows but that it may be the shoot from which, a time hence, there may spring many cabins, then finer homes, and buildings, and mansions, until at last there is a great, brave city here on this port by the delta—"

"That's it, Pop!" said Dick suddenly. "There's the name for our settlement. Delta Port!"

So, swiftly, sped the next weeks, and Bobby was not able, afterward, to tell where they had gone. Time lightens labor; labor hastens time. But fleeing hours left in their wake tangible evidence of their passage—a change, a growth in Delta Port.

One of Pop's first moves had been an attempted reorganization of their work-hours on an Eros basis.

"We cannot here," he explained, "try to maintain our Earthly habit of sleeping through night hours, working during the day. Therefore—"

And he laid out for them an intricate and elaborate "nine day week" he had devised; broken into alternate sleep-and-labor, meal-and-recreation periods. It was an ingenious system. But—

It didn't work.

Despite previous habits, after a short time men and women, old and young alike, found themselves growing drowsy as dusk crept in. There was a general quickening of life's tempo to meet the conditions prevalent on Eros; the familiar "three meals a day" ceased to have meaning; the old habit of sleeping eight hours at one stretch became anomalous under a sky which waxed and waned from brightness to dark in that length of time. Imperceptibly at first, then more and more openly, all found themselves working into a new routine. A design for living under which they tumbled into bed for four hours of darkness, slept suddenly and heartily, woke again, pursued a half dozen hours of work or play, then napped once more.

It seemed the most natural thing in the world. And Pop, never satisfied until he could explain such things, finally found an answer.

"I remember, now, that 'way back in the early years of the Twentieth Century a group of psychologists from one of the American universities tried an experiment. They put two men in a sealed, walled, sound-proof room which was neither dark nor light, but was kept constantly a dull, twilight gray.

"They gave the men—who all their lives had lived on the accepted Early standard—instructions to sleep when they felt drowsy, eat whenever they felt the desire to do so. After an exceptionally short time, the life-habits of these human guinea-pigs altered remarkably. They began eating not thrice a way, but at intervals ranging from every three to six hours.

"As for sleeping, the experimenters found it natural to cat-nap for four hour stretches rather than sustain strength on one, long, tiresome eight hour sleep-period.

"This experiment was duplicated in 1987, under John Carberry of Columbia, with identical results. The research doctors were forced to the conclusion that Man is, on Earth, responsive to the conditions under which he must live. That is, he has adapted himself to Earth's phenomena. But could his body attain its natural and normal, uninhibited desires, it would live *precisely as we here on Eros are living!* At a wake-sleep pace of alternate four and six hours!"

It was just like Pop to get excited about a problem of that nature when there were so many other things crying to be done. But Bobby was surprised, from time to time, to discover that in a pinch Pop could bob up with an answer to a stumping question quite unrelated to the field of empiric science.

It was Pop who, when Dick was having trouble making their

minute supply of nails and braces do for the construction of the cabin, offered the suggestion that the joists be joined by hollowing. It worked. End logs dove-tailed beautifully; the cabin walls stood firmer and looked neater than if laboriously spliced together with metal.

It was Pop, too, who did something about the plate problem. Unable to bring the plastics with them in their hasty flight from the sunken *Cuchulainn*, the Moseley family had made rude shift first with large flat, washed leaves, then with shells taken from the beach, at last with wooden slabs planed down by Grampaw.

Pop, annoyed with these slovenly substitutes, spent several hours wandering by the shore, through the hills, up the river; finally returned one afternoon triumphantly bearing a lump of grayish mud as large as his head. Ignoring all caustic queries and comments, he set about molding this into a plate—and after much fingering, succeeded in flattening it into a recognizable shape.

It seemed to bother him not a whit that the finished product was deckle-edged and wobbly. He set it out in the sun to dry; a day later carried it triumphantly to the table and demanded his meal be served in it.

"Pottery!" he said. "From a fine clay bed up Erin River!"

Then he placed his pottery plate on the table with firm hands, and at that imperceptible jar, it promptly fell into five pieces!

But a beginning had been made, and curiously enough it was Moira who became interested in this obscure art of ceramics. The Moseleys continued to eat from wooden slabs for some weeks, while Moira begrimed her fingers with mud that invariably turned to crisp, fragile clay—and then one day she completed a bowl made of substance from which all sand-grains and small pebbles had been painstakingly sieved, and which had been allowed to dry slowly under damp grass. And *this* time it did not crack. Within a fortnight, a complete set of crockery made its appearance in the culinary department.

At which point Dick began talking vaguely about the construction of a kiln, and Moira started thinking about the possibilities of decorating her proud young chinaware.

So the weeks passed, and it was surprising how much had been accomplished, and how complete and happy life could be, even without the infinitude of small comforts to which they had once been accustomed, and which, on Earth, they had expected and accepted unthinkingly.

There was no teleo to entertain them, but somehow nobody seemed to miss its raucous, glowing presence in the living room; not even Bobby whose greatest interest in life had once been the nightly adventures of *The Red Patrolman*, transmitted through the courtesy of United Syntho Cereals. Grampaw Moseley made music with a battered banjo he had salvaged from the *Cuchulainn*; they all sang, and sometimes they danced, too. That was what Moira liked; she'd fix herself all up real pretty and dance and dance, even though her partners were Dick and Pop, who didn't dance the modern swoop-steps very well, and Bobby, who pretended to dislike it very thoroughly, but thought it was kind of fun.

Grampaw carved a cribbage set, too; they played it, and chess, and card games during storms that kept them housebound. Dick, in occasional hours of leisure, cleared a fair athletic field outside. They had a quoits' run, a badminton court (a little uneven, but nobody minded) and a shuffleboard plane; also a fine sand-pit for The Pooch.

Pop had planned the house with his usual mathematical forevision. From its first two rooms, built with an eye to offering swift shelter, soon spread wings. Before long it had four separate bedrooms, a kitchen, a dining-nook, and the living- or meeting-room, which Grampaw called the "git-together" room. There was also a cisterned refreshing-room, and another would be added as soon as Dick devised a method of supplying the house with fresh, running water.

Meanwhile, Mom and Eleanor and Grampaw Moseley were to be thanked for the steady improvement in their menu.

Grampaw had early set out his farm; it was a sight to see him hobbling up and down the neat, even rows, weeding his springing crops, swearing at insect interlopers. Luckily the sealed containers of seeds had not suffered the fate of Mom's lamented sugar and flour supply; the Moseleys had already nibbled tentatively at stubby radishes, tiny, crumpled leaves of lettuce—and in another month or so there would be more substantial root and fruit stocks. Potatoes, parsnips, beans, turnips, beets, tomatoes, corn, salsify, onions.

And wheat! That was the crop most tenderly watched, most hopefully awaited. Wheat meant bread; bread was life. And the wheat was rippling up in soft, green wavelets.

Meanwhile, Eros itself supplied many—if unusual!—foodstuffs. Every member of the family watched, carefully, the eating habits of Erosian small-life; adapted to their own diet the fruits, seeds, berries, eaten by native animals, and avoided those things which, no matter how luscious to look on, the birds and beasts eschewed. Some day, when Pop's laboratory equipment could be brought from the sunken ship, they would find out about these questionable foods. But for now, it was best to be on the safe side.

Artificial light remained a problem. There were tiny search batteries in their bulgers, but they used these only in cases of necessity; they had no oil for lamps even if they had owned lamps. Eleanor made a few fat, greasy, ill-shapen candles out of renderings, but these spluttered and dripped and lasted but a short time. Aboard the *Cuchulainn* were all sorts of books, telling how to make candles properly. But these were, by now, water-soaked and illegible.

So they contrived to get by with little illumination, looking forward to the day when Dick should succeed in raising the hypatomic motor from the ship. Then they would have all the light and heat and power they wanted. All from a cupful of water, or a handful of sand swept up from the beach.

And all was peaceful and quiet. Until one day there came a startled shout from the fields, the sound of excited footsteps, and Grampaw came hobbling into the house yelling, "Where's m' gun? Marthy, drad-rat it, where'd y' put m' gun?"

Dick grinned and winked at the others and asked, "What's the matter, Grampaw? The moles getting into your garden?" And chuckled as Grampaw grabbed up his pierce-gun and hobbled away. Chuckled, that is, until the old man's answer came floating back over his shoulder.

"Moles be durned! It's hooman-bein's, that's what it is. *In*-trudin' on our prop-pity!"

Then Dick roared, "Hey, Grampaw, wait! Put that gun down! Don't try to—Come on, everyone!"

They all went tumbling from the house. And it was exactly as Grampaw had said. Approaching Delta Port, some on foot, some astride animals curiously horselike save that they had six legs and long, shaggy hair, came a tiny group of men and women. Six in number.

Their leader was a man of Pop's age, a baldish man, heavy-set and capable looking. Besides him rode a thin, tired looking woman of forty-odd. Next came a short, pudgy, white-haired man; then, herding beside him two youngsters, a boy of Bobby's age and a girl slightly younger, came the last member of the party. A slim, tall young man with a mop of cinnamon-colored hair.

The two groups, one nearing the house, one emerging from it, saw each other at practically the same time. For a moment, no one spoke on either side. Dick had taken the gun from Grampaw's hands, had successfully concealed it. And now Pop broke the silence.

"Greetings, strangers!" he cried heartily. "You're plenty welcome to Delta Port!"

Then came the shockingly unexpected reply, from the leader of the newcomers.

"Greetings yourself, Mister! And what in tarnation thunder are you doing on my land?"

IV

Grampaw Moseley was a man of action. He groped for the rifle swinging loosely in Dick's grasp. He said, "Gimme! Minute I set eyes on that fat ol' popinjay I knew—"

Dick said, "Hush, Grampaw!" and looked at Pop. Pop looked baffled. He watched speechlessly as the caravan drew up beside them, the members dismounted from their odd beasts of burden. Then he said, hesitantly, "There seems to be some misunderstanding here, stranger. Allow me to introduce myself and my family. I am Robert Moseley. This is my father, my wife, my son and his wife and child, my other children—"

The heavy-set man made no offer to shake hands. He grunted, "Meetcha! I'm Sam Wilkes. This is my wife, my dad, my kids." He stared at the house, the cultivated fields. A look of grudging respect was in his eyes; there was a touch of envy, too. "Been doin' all right for yourself, ain't you? For a squatter!"

Pop said slowly, "Squatter, sir? I'm afraid there's some mistake. This property—as a matter of fact, this entire planetoid—is mine under Earth land-grant law. Now, if you will be kind enough to explain your presence—"

"Yours!" Sam Wilkes' ruddy countenance darkened with outrage. "Earth land-grant! Bessie, where'd I put that—Oh, here it is! Take a look at this, Mr. Moseley!"

He slapped a strip of parchment into Pop's hand, and Pop unfolded it carefully. Dick looked over his shoulder. One of the curious, six-legged beasts skittered nervously and Bobby started. The rusty-thatched boy who had dismounted from it grinned impishly. He said, "What's the matter, skinny, you scared of him?"

Bobby said, "Of course not!" and watched the animal from the corner of one eye. "What is it?"

"A gooldak. We brought it here from home. Fastest thing on legs. What's your name?"

"Bobby. What's yours? And what do you mean—home?"

"Sam. They call me Junior. Why, home is Mars, of course. Where'd you think?"

That word was being echoed now by Dick.

"Mars! This is a land-grant charter issued by the Martian government! But—but—Pop, show him yours!"

"Don't do nothin' of the sort, son!" chirped Grampaw belligerently. "That there scrip o' his'n is prob'ly fake! Don't explain nothin' to 'em. Jist tell 'em to git!"

The roly-poly father of Sam Wilkes turned a querulous eye on Grampaw.

"Who's the antique?" he demanded throatily. "Sounds to me like one of them big-talkin', poor-scrappin' Earth soldiers I fit in the Upland Rebellion."

"Upland Rebellion!" howled Grampaw. "Was *you* one o' the rebels we chased from the deserts to the Pole? I might of knowed it! Gimme that gun, Dick—"

"Please, Grampaw!" begged Dick. He looked at Wilkes. "My father was right, Mr. Wilkes. There is a dreadful mistake here. Apparently the Colonial offices of Earth and Mars have disagreed on the ownership of this planetoid; your government has issued a land-grant on it, and so has ours."

"Asteroids," said Wilkes, "are Martian. Their very orbits prove—"

"I beg your pardon," interrupted Pop firmly. "Eros' orbit is between Earth and Mars at this moment. It is a part of Earth's empire."

"Is it true," Bobby asked Junior, wide-eyed, "that pirate gangs hide in the Martian deserts? I heard—"

"Shucks, no! We used to live in East Redlands, they wasn't no pirates anywheres about. Were you ever in Chicago, Skinny? Is it true there's a building there two miles high?"

"Two and a half," said Bobby complacently. "And it covers six city blocks. And my name's not 'Skinny'."

"—you'll notice," Wilkes was grunting, "my grant is dated prior to yours. Therefore Eros is mine, no matter which government's claim is soundest. That's Intergalactic law."

"You seem to forget," Dick pointed out, "that we've established a permanent settlement. As travelers, you may be considered itinerant explorers with only the privileges of a study party. We will extend to you the courtesies of Eros for the legal three months, but after that time—"

"*You'll* extend to *us*!" Wilkes' face was flame-red. "Why, for a lead credit, I'd—"

"Sock 'im, Dick!" yelped Grampaw excitedly. "Don't let 'im git away with that talk! Sock 'im!"

"Nobody," rumbled a deep, pleasant voice, "is going to sock anybody." The tall, elder son of Sam Wilkes ranged himself beside his father. Bobby noted with sudden approval that the young man's bronzed forearms were corded; there was a crisp, firm set to his lips; he looked like a man who could handle himself equally well in a ball-room or a brawl. He said, "Send the women away, Mr. Moseley. I think we men can settle this matter."

Moira stepped forward, confronted the young redhead boldly. "And who are *you* to be giving orders to us? Maybe Martians treat their women like cattle, but Earthmen—"

"That will do, daughter," said Pop. And he nodded. "But that's not a bad idea, Wilkes. There is no reason why we should not be able to settle this question in a friendly manner. Mrs. Wilkes, if you and your daughter would accept our hospitality, I'm sure Martha can find you a cup of tea. Wilkes, if you and your son would care to sit down with us, we can—Bobby, run and get some water for the Wilkes' horses. If they are horses?" he added dubiously.

"Gooldaks!" sniffed Junior Wilkes disdainfully. "I'll help you, Skinny. What's the matter with that sister of yours? She looks like an unbaked cookie."

"Yeah? Then why does your brother keep staring at her all the time? Come on—" Bobby strained desperately for a suitable term; culled his resources, came up triumphantly. "Come on, Stinky!"

When they had watered and fed the gooldaks, Junior wanted to see around the farm. Bobby showed him, while the other boy marveled wistfully.

"You folks struck it lucky. This is the best part of the whole planet.... I mean of what we've seen so far. We got here a couple weeks before you did, and we've traveled a couple hundred miles looking for a good location. Boy, it sure was awful where we cracked up! Dad named it Little Hell, because it's so hot and sandy and terrible. No fresh water. One big hot, salt lake. Red mountains and desert land. All oxides, Red said—he's my brother. He's smart."

"So's mine," said Bobby. "Are Martians people?"

"What do you mean? Of course they're people. Same as you. Men that left Earth because there was too darn much fighting and stuff. And of course Earth tried to claim Mars as a colony, but Mars won its fight for independence."

"Earth just let 'em go free," scoffed Bobby. "They didn't want any dried-up old planet, anyhow!"

"No? Then why did they—Hey! What's that?"

"Quoits. Know how?"

"Do I! I can beat you!"

"Huh!" said Bobby. He glanced at the house, but no one was paying any attention to them. Pop and Dick were deep in conversation with the Wilkes, father and son. The two old men were aside on one corner of the porch rubbing salt in old wounds, re-fighting the battles of Mercandor's Canal and High Plateau, re-surveying the campaigns that had led to Martian independence and a better understanding between the blue and red planets. Eleanor and Mom were preparing dinner; Moira had disappeared. A thin and lonely figure stood on the steps looking at Bobby and Junior. Junior called, "Hey, Ginger—come on down if you want to." She came.

Bobby said, "What did you call her for?"

"What's the matter? You 'fraid a girl can lick you playing games?"

"Huh!" said Bobby again. There was something sissy about playing games with fourteen-year-old girls. It didn't help much that Ginger, with skinny-armed, keen-eyed accuracy succeeded in beating both himself and her brother in two games of quoits and one of shuffleboard before the dinner-gong rang.

Dinner was a truculent experience. Conversation had done absolutely nothing to clarify the issue. Both parties were sincere in their conviction of ownership to Eros. Pop based his claim on the establishment of a permanent base at Delta Port; Wilkes insisted that priority of arrival was his proof of occupancy.

"So one of us," insisted Wilkes, "has got to leave. And since *we* can't—"

"Can't?"

"Our ship crashed," explained Red Wilkes, watching Moira, "on landing. It is a total wreck."

Bobby thought, glumly, that Moira was a total wreck, too. He had held hopes for Moira. Since their arrival on Eros she had turned into a pretty nice guy; cheerful, willing to work, fresh-looking. Now, for some obscure reason, she had piled her hair up on top of her head, put powder on her face and red stuff on her mouth. She wore a dress instead of pants, and she was mincing and prissing around like a prize horse.

"So," continued Wilkes, "since *we* can't leave, your family must."

And Dick laughed out loud.

"Checkmate!" he said.

"What?"

"We've wasted time," said Dick, "trying to decide which family must leave. The truth is, neither of us can! Because, you see, we cracked up in landing, also. Our ship lies out there four fathoms deep in Delta Sound!" He rose. "So that's that, folks. And I'm afraid, Mr. Wilkes, that under the present circumstances, *your* family will be the one to ultimately depart from Eros."

"Ours? Why?"

"Because of the internationally recognized laws of squatters' rights. You must know the requirements a settler has to fulfill in order to establish claim to land? He must declare his purpose of settling upon leaving the parent planet—"

"We did that," said Red Wilkes, "before we left."

"I know. And four months later he will be visited by an inspection ship of the S.S.P.—"

"We know that, too."

"—upon the arrival of which," Dick continued, "he must show advancement in the following colonization projects. (a) Establishment of a power plant or unit; (b) construction of a suitable dwelling or dwellings; (c) satisfactory advancement of natural resources, including farms, fisheries or other means of livelihood and sustenance—"

"Get to the point!" growled Wilkes.

"Immediately. And with pleasure. You see, my dear sir, as you have told us, you left Mars even *before* we left Earth. But whereas we have turned our time to good account, constructing the comforts which you now see about you, your family has squandered precious weeks wandering over the face of Eros seeking a favorable location.

"If I am not mistaken, the Solar Space Patrol's inspection is only six short weeks in the offing. And judging from our experience, you cannot possibly satisfy the requirements of the land-grant code in that short space of time. I remind you that the planting of a garden would, in itself, spell an end to your ambitions."

Sam Wilkes was on his feet, choking with rage.

"That there law is nonsense, Moseley! The land law allows us a full year to establish a settlement—"

"Ah, yes! The land law. But you forget that these are unusual circumstances. Two families with equally valid rights have claimed Eros. Land law is overruled, and the law of squatters' dominion comes into effect.

"So, I'm very sorry for you, Wilkes. But I hope we can be friendly neighbors for the short time you *remain* here with us on Eros."

Wilkes was a statue of dismay. The rigidity of him melted enough to let him turn slowly to his son.

"Is—is that right, Red?"

And the younger Wilkes nodded.

"I'm afraid it is, Dad."

Sam Wilkes brought his fist down on the table. The hand-made crockery danced and trembled.

"Then, by Gad! I'll have no more of this talk or no more phoney hospitality. Bessie, Ginger, Papa—come on! We're getting out of here! We've got work to do!"

Pop said slowly, "I'm sorry, Wilkes. But—"

"Sorry! Bah!"

"And just where," cackled Grampaw, loving it, "might y' be goin'?"

"Not far. Right across the river. You can't claim all of this fertile valley—yet! And you haven't cleared that ground."

He stomped to the door; turned there for one, final warning.

"—and I advise you Moseleys to keep off our land, too! We're goin' to be mighty busy provin' our right to own this planet. I understand there's pests around these parts that are darn disturbin'; I'd hate to make a mistake and shoot any skunks by accident. Come on, Mama!"

Bessie Wilkes looked at Mom. Her worn, tired features sagged piteously. She wet her lips. "Mrs. Moseley—"

Mom said, "Rob, don't you think you're being a little harsh, maybe?"

But there was a streak of granite in Pop, too. And he was angry; white-angry as only a tried Irishman can be. He said in a cold and level voice, "I think, Mother, you should get Mrs. Wilkes' wraps."

And they left. Ginger Wilkes turned to stick out her tongue at Bobby as they got on their gooldaks and rode toward the river. And Junior made a gesture which Bobby returned in kind. But Red Wilkes didn't even look back. So there was no good reason why Moira should have suddenly burst into tears and gone to her own room....

V

—

It was Dick who brought home the bad news. Two Eros days had passed since the Wilkes took their angry departure from the Moseley home. In those two days, an unhappy atmosphere had settled down over the house at Delta Port. Moira said little or nothing, Mom just moped around the house, The Pooch got indigestion and cried interminably; even Grampaw Moseley was grumpier than usual. Bobby tried to forget the depression by playing quoits. He gave it up as a bad job. It wasn't any fun playing by yourself, and Dick and Pop were too busy to play with him. If only—

But comets to Junior Wilkes! And Ginger, too!

At dinner time, Dick came into the house slowly, a thoughtful look in his eyes. When they were seated he said, suddenly, "Have any of you seen the Wilkes lately?"

Grampaw said, "I seen Old Man Wilkes. He was pitchforkin' land down by our south forty, oney on the opposite side o' the river. Fat ol' sinner. I chucked a rock at 'im!"

Bobby looked interested.

"You hit him, Grampaw?"

"I don't never miss. In the right leg."

"I bet he hollered."

Grampaw sucked his upper plate fiercely. "Nary a holler, durn him! He jist pulled up his pants-leg and made a face at me. *De*-crepit ol' fool's got a wooden leg!"

Pop said, "Why did you ask, Richard?"

"I was wondering if any of you had noticed what I did."

"What do you mean?"

Dick started to answer, stopped, rose. "Come," he said. "It's dark. I'll show you."

They followed him out to the porch. From there the Wilkes settlement could not ordinarily be seen. Which is why, as they stood there, one and all gasped astonishment.

The thick, black Erosian night lay heavy about them every-where except in the direction of the Wilkes' new home. There it was light; startlingly, dazzlingly, brilliantly gay and bright! Like a great white dawn on the river's edge.

"Power!" cried Pop. "Atomic power! They must have a hypatomic!"

"They never said they hadn't. They told us their spaceship cracked up; we just took it for granted that since we hadn't been able to salvage our hypatomic, neither could they."

Bobby said wonderingly, "Gee, Pop, it looks like at home, doesn't it? I forgot lights were so bright."

Pop said, "I'm afraid we've underestimated our competitors, son. If they have power, they can accomplish all we have, and more! And in one-tenth the time."

"That's just," said Dick slowly, "what I'm afraid of. There's only one answer to this challenge. I've *got* to get our hypatomic from the *Cuchulainn*. And quickly."

"But you said—"

"I know what I said. But I also know what they can do. In three days they can have a house ... a fine, big, plastic house that will make our hand-hewn log cabin look like a cowshed. They'll have electricity, fuel, running water, all the things we've had to do without. When the inspectors see their house and compare it with ours—Mom—get me my bulger. I'm leaving for the north shore."

"Tonight, Richard?"

"Immediately."

Pop said, "And Bobby and I will go with you."

They were there before morning. The A shore looked much as Bobby remembered it, except that now there was a raft there; the craft which Dick had used to float out to the sunken ship on previous visits. The three of them boarded this, paddled out to the bobbing buoy that marked the *Cuchulainn's* watery resting-place.

Dick donned his bulger, weighted his boots, and went below. The sun rose higher in the east. After a while, green wavelets rolled and Dick was up again.

"It's no use, Pop. It's like I said. The ship has continued to settle; the airlock is jammed tight against the bottom. I can't get in any more."

Pop said, "And I suppose there's no way to attach a drag to the ship, work it loose?"

"It would take more power than we have." Gloomily.

And then Bobby remembered, suddenly. He said, "Hey, Dick—!"

"Never mind, kid. Help me off with this suit."

"But listen, Dick. I read a story once—"

"Do what your brother asks, Robert."

"Will you let me finish, Pop? Listen, Dick, in this story a rocketeer got locked out of his spaceship. So he unfastened the stern-braces and got in through the rocket jet!"

"He ... did ... what?"

"Unfastened the stern-braces—"

"I heard you!" Dick's face had suddenly lighted. "Great day in the morning, Pop—I bet it'll work! Hand me that jack-wrench ... that's the one! So long!"

And he was under water again. This time he stayed under for more than an hour. He bobbed up, finally, while Pop and Bobby were having sandwiches. Pop said, "How's it going, Richard?"

"Give me a fresh capsule," demanded Dick. He took the oxy-tainer, replenished his supply pack, disappeared. A long time passed. Too long a time. Bobby began to feel apprehensive. He didn't say anything, though, because he knew Pop was feeling the same way. And then—

"There he is!" said Pop. And sure enough, Dick was coming up out of the water slowly. Terribly slowly. Bobby saw why. It was because he was weighted by a square box held in his arms. A familiar square box. The hypatomic motor of the *Cuchulainn*!

"Got it!" gasped Dick. "Easy, now ... it's heavy. I hope it'll work. It's been under water so doggoned long—"

Joyfully, they lugged it all the way back to Delta Port. It was sleep-time when they got there, but they were too excited to sleep. By fire- and candle-light, Dick worked on the salvaged power unit, patching, wiring, repairing. And at dawn he had it hooked up. He raised his head gleefully.

"Get ready, folks! Here's the blow that smashes the hopes of the Wilkes clan. Behold—*light*!"

And he closed a switch. There was a throbbing hum, a glow, a moment of bright, joyous, welcome light. Then an angry growl from deep in the bowels of the atomic box. And a sudden, blinding flash of blue light—

Darkness! And from the darkness, Pop's voice.

"Ruined! It was under water too long, son. Too long!"

"Too long," echoed Dick dolefully.

It was Grampaw Moseley who revived their dejected spirits. When they had rested, he came to them, pounding his cane on the floor, snarling at them with unexpected vigor.

"You young uns gimme a pain! Robert, I'm ashamed o' ye. An' you, too, Dicky-boy! Actin' like we was licked just because a silly-lookin' little old box won't act up right.

"We was gettin' along fine here without no atomic motor, wasn't we? Buildin' a friendly, comf'table community? Well, why can't we go on livin' like we was? We'll solve the heat an' light problem some other way, that's all!"

Pop said, "I know, Father. But in time? After all, when the inspectors come—"

"Inspectors my foot! They's one thing we got that the dad-blamed Wilkes can't git with all their heat an' free power an' hot-an'-cold runnin' water, ain't they?"

"Wh-what's that?"

"Vittles! One o' the requirements is the settler's got to git him a garden growin', ain't it? Well, we got one. An' the Wilkes ain't. An', dag-nab it, they ain't goin' to grow wheat an' tomateys an' butter-beans out of a metal box! So stop belly-achin' and git back to work, the two of ye!"

His words were harsh, but the bitter medicine cured the ill. There was truth in what he said. So, putting behind them all dreams of motorized accomplishment, the Moseley family once more returned to the task of making complete and comfortable their home at Delta Port.

Dick tackled once more the problem of running water for their home. This time he solved it with the aid of Grampaw's capable cooperage. A huge tank, set into the eaves, stored the water. A hand-pump drew it from the stream. An old, hollow brass doorknob, pierced with drill-holes, secured to the end of the 'fresher pipe, made an excellent spray for the shower.

Grampaw worked his farm ferociously; Mom and Eleanor and Moira spent hours in the kitchen, jarring and preserving the produce he was now harvesting. Bobby's chores piled up till it seemed he had scarcely any time left for playing. He was enjoying himself, though. It was fun feeling that his efforts were helping toward putting the Wilkes where they belonged.

Moira seemed to be thriving on this pioneer life, too. She had developed a sudden love for the country; even after a hard day's work she would set out, almost every evening, for a tramp about the countryside. She didn't show very good sense about it, though, for like as not she'd go out all be-doodled up in a dress and high-heeled shoes, and come back flushed and excited and hardly caring that she was ruining her best clothes.

Once Bobby decided to go walking with her, but she slipped away before he could announce his intention. He lost her down by the river-bank, and since an hour of sun and dusk remained, decided to go swimming. He had been in the water but a few minutes when the brush parted and there was Junior Wilkes.

"Hello," said Junior.

"Hello, yourself," said Bobby.

Junior said, "I'm looking for Red."

"Well, he's not here." Bobby continued paddling. The brush crackled and he thought Stinky had gone. He looked up, suddenly feeling loneliness close in upon him. But the other boy was still there. He was hesitantly fumbling at his shirt-buttons. Bobby said, "You can come in if you want to. I guess this river don't belong to nobody."

They swam together for quite a while, neither wanting to break the silence. It would be, thought Bobby vaguely, an act of disloyalty. To Pop and Dick and the family. Of course, if Junior spoke first....

When they were dressing, each on his own side of the river, Junior spoke. He said, "You ever play quoits any more?"

"All the time," said Bobby airily. He hadn't laid a hand on the quoits since that afternoon. "We have a lot of fun," he said.

"Well, so do we," said Junior. He added, "Anyway, I can have your quoits' run after you leave Eros. My Dad said so."

"Don't hold your breath waiting," snorted Bobby. "I guess I'll be living in your big house after you go away."

"It's a nicer house than yours!"

"Did I say it wasn't?" Bobby had seen it. It was a beauty. But why not, with the limitless power of an atomic machine to supply the labor of creating plastic, operate the lifts and perform all the hard manual labor? "You ought to see our garden, though. We've got corn and beans and all sorts of things."

"No kidding?" Junior looked hungry. But he shook his head. "Synthos suit me *exactly*! I'd rather eat them than any home-grown stuff."

"I bet!" scoffed Bobby. He had finished dressing. He turned awkwardly. "Well—see you!" he said.

"Tomorrow night," said Junior. And, shucks, that was a date. He couldn't break it, after that, even if he had only been being polite. And it sort of got to be a habit to swim together for a little while every evening. He didn't tell Pop because Pop would be mad. And Junior didn't tell his old man, because he knew he'd get whaled....

And the weeks raced by on eager feet. Until one day, shortly after breakfast, Bobby went out to see how clear the weather was, so he could go fishing; looked heavenward—and came racing back into the house.

"Pop!" he yelled. "Dick! A ship! I think it's the Patrol ship. Coming here!"

They came running. And it was the Patrol ship. It circled high above them like a giant eagle, then, with a flat, flooding thunder of jet-fire, dropped to rest in a field between the properties of the two feuding clans.

VI

The commander of the Patrolship *Sirius* was Lt.-Col. Travers, third ranking officer of the Belt Fleet. He shook Pop's hand heartily.

"Glad to meet you, Dr. Moseley. I've heard so much about you, I feel as if I already know you. My nephew was a student in several of your classes at Midland U. He said you were a very capable instructor ... and if I may judge from what we noted from above, I might add that you are an extremely capable colonist as well as professor."

Pop wriggled. "Why—why, thank you, Colonel."

"This fine farmland," smiled the space officer, "and that artesian well I see across the river ... these silos, and your magnificent dwelling...."

Pop hrrumphed, even more embarrassed.

"Colonel," he faltered, "I think I'd better explain immediately that all is not mine. There are two groups of claimants to this planetoid. Ourselves and a family named Wilkes. Martians. Our property is here; theirs is across the river. I—uh—here comes Wilkes now."

Travers' brow furrowed.

"Indeed? Then he was right, after all!"

"He? Who?"

The question was answered by the appearance of a man in drill space-gear who stepped from the *Sirius*. A lean and capable-appearing man, hard-bitten of feature, shrewd of eye and tight of lip.

Colonel Travers said, "Dr. Moseley, permit me to introduce Mr. Wade, survey scout of the United Ores Corporation."

Wade acknowledged the introduction with a crisp nod. Then, "What's this about there being two claimants to Eros?" He turned to the ship's commander. "This makes a difference, doesn't it, Colonel? My information was correct. Therefore it becomes your duty to make a final, exhaustive study of the settlers' accomplishments right *now*. And in the event their projects have not been completed in accordance with the provisions of the Squatter's Rights Code, Section 103A, Paragraphs vii to xix, inclusive—"

Eleanor whispered nervously, "What does he mean, Dick? What is he talking about?" and Dick nodded tightly. "I think I know." He stepped forward. "I take it, Mr. Wade, that the U.O.C. has filed a claim on the possession of Eros in the event that our settlement projects should not satisfy the inspector's requirements?"

"Quite right, young man. And I might add—" Wade was openly hostile. "I might add that I have obtained permission to accompany Colonel Travers on his inspection tour. In order to verify his findings. If I am not satisfied—"

"That will do, Mr. Wade!" Colonel Travers was under orders to treat his passenger as a guest; there was no obligation that he like the ore scout. The glint in his eye, the set of his jaw, indicated the direction in which his sympathy lay. "I am quite capable of handling this. Ah—Good day, sir! Mr. Wilkes, I presume?"

"Howdy, Skipper. Yeah, I'm Sam Wilkes." The rival settler glanced around swiftly, sensed the overtones of enmity, glared at Pop suspiciously. "What's wrong here? Has Moseley been squawkin' about—?"

"Dr. Moseley informed us that you and he were both claimants to Eros. Therefore I shall immediately visit your two establishments in order to determine which, if either of you, has the better justified his claim.

"Lieutenant Thrainell, you will serve as my aide. We will first inspect Dr. Moseley's habitation."

Thus it began. Pop took the two Patrolmen and the civilian critic to Delta Port, pointed out with pride the many things accomplished within the past months. He met, in Col. Travers, an admiring audience. The commander was outspokenly delighted with what he saw.

"Gad, man! You did all this without power? This is the pioneering feat of the decade! Look, Lieutenant! Running water ... chinaware ... that furniture! Marvelous! You deserve a wealth of credit, Doctor."

"But," pointed out Wade caustically, "you mentioned the biggest fault yourself."

"I beg your pardon, Mr. Wade?"

"Without power!" snapped Wade. "Moseley, where are your lights? Where's your power plant? How about heat? And this cooking equipment—it's aboriginal!"

Pop said stiffly, "We have no hypatomic, sir. But you will notice that we have devised satisfactory substitutes for power-driven gear. Hand-pumps draw our water, light is supplied by these oil-float lamps, our house is centrally heated by these open fire-places. We are—" He faltered. "We shall, of course, order a complete hypatomic unit from Earth, install it as soon as possible."

"I'm afraid that's not quick enough," sneered Wade. "Colonel Travers will undoubtedly remember the requirements of the law in that respect. 'Claimant must display, at time of inspection, a power-plant of atomic, motor, or hydraulic drive capable of generating a minimum of 3,000 Legerling units *per diem*, and so arranged as to provide dwellings and other structures with heat, light and power.' You have no such equipment, have you, Dr. Moseley?"

"No, but—"

"You have not, then?"

"No."

"Very well, then." Wade smiled thinly, closed the black book in which he had been jotting notes with a plushy sound of finality. "May I suggest, Colonel, that we see the *other* claimant's plantation?"

After they had left, Colonel Travers shaking his head regretfully at Pop as if to say he was sorry but helpless before the arguments of this interloper, Pop sat down and propped his chin on his fists. Yesterday he had looked like a man of thirty; all of sudden he looked old and weary and discouraged. He said, "Well, there it is, Martha. I've dreamed my dream, and now it's over, and I've failed."

"No you haven't Rob. The Colonel is on our side. He's a good man. He'll—"

"But the law is on Wade's side. If our claim is outlawed, Eros will become a dirty, smoky mining camp. This soft beauty, these green rolling hills, will echo with the clatter of blasters. Unless—"

And suddenly he was again a man of action. He came to his feet suddenly.

"Martha, Eleanor, Dick—everybody! Get those preserves out of the storage closet. Grampaw, get the hauler from the shed. Bobby, you run and tell Sam Wilkes to keep those inspectors out of his house for a half hour or so."

"Why, Pop?" demanded Dick. "What are you going to do?"

"Do? I'm going to see that Sam Wilkes gets this planet, that's what! Oh, I know—there won't be any question of his sharing it with me. He's too hard and stiff-necked a man for that. But he's our kind of man, with all his faults. A pioneer with the daring to come to a new world and try to build it into a home of his own.

"We've known for weeks that all he needed to justify his claim was a food supply. Well, by thunder, we've got a food supply! And we'll give it to him, lock, stock and barrel, to keep Eros out of the Corporation's hands! Now, step, everybody! Moira! Moira—where is that girl?"

"She stayed down by the river, Pop."

"Well, find her. Bobby, go tell Sam Wilkes what I just said!"

Bobby scooted.

He was soaking wet when he got to the Wilkes' house. That was because he took the short-cut, which meant plunging right into the river and swimming across, clothes and all. The inspectors and their snoopy companion would have to take the long route, around the ford.

Mr. Wilkes wasn't in the house when he got there. But Mrs. Wilkes was, and Ginger, and both gasped as they saw him. Mrs. Wilkes bustled forward.

"Sweet stars above, child, what are you doing here? Get those clothes off; you'll catch your death of cold. Ginger—go get one of Junior's suits—"

Bobby said, "There's no time for that, Mrs. Wilkes. Where's Fat Sa—I mean, where's your husband?"

Ginger said, "Don't tell him, Ma. He's just here to crow because he knows we can't pass the inspection requirements—"

"You—you shut up!" bellowed Bobby. "You doggone female! You don't know anything about it. Mrs. Wilkes, get your husband. Mom and Sis and the rest will be here any minute now. They're—"

And he explained. His explanation sent them into a flurry of excitement; there was even deeper excitement when Sam Wilkes, hastily summoned, heard the same story repeated. For once the leathery corners of his mouth relaxed into something like a grin. He swore, and slammed a big hand on his knee.

"Your old man is going to do that for us, sonny? Well, hornswoggle my jets! And to think I—Junior, go find Red. Hop it!"

"Red's not around, Pa. He went toward the river."

"Confound him! Just when we need him most. Well—I'll go meet the confounded rascals, stall them as long as I can. And look here, you—what's your name?"

"Bobby."

"I won't forget this, Bobby! Not by a jugfull. If I hadn't been such a stubborn, pigheaded old hound, I'd have dickered with your Pa long afore this. There's plenty of room on Eros for two families. Or two dozen!"

Then followed a half hour of labor so swift that it made all the accomplishments of the past months seem snail-like by comparison. Mom and Eleanor arrived, bearing armloads of canned goods and preserves; Grampaw and Dick brought the hauler across the river on a raft, and piled high on the hauler were fresh vegetables that gorged the never-used Wilkes containers to repletion. It was fast work, but efficient. And when, about three-quarters of an Earth hour later, Wilkes came from the lower acreage accompanied by the two officers and the Corporation investigator, the job was finished, and a tired but glowing two-family group awaited him.

Colonel Travers' inspection of the food-supply was perfunctory. It needed not be otherwise. One glance sufficed to show that there was in the Wilkes household enough food to nourish a dozen families for as many months.

And there was a smile of grim satisfaction on his lips as,

turning to his aide, he said, "Very well, Lieutenant. You may make a notation that the Wilkes household has been inspected and found satisfactory in all respects." He looked at Wade purposefully and repeated in a firm tone. "In *all* respects!"

Ah, he was no dummy, that Colonel. Bobby had seen the twinkle in his eye as he glanced into the preserve closet. Because, shucks! there wasn't any mistaking Mom's way of doing up preserves. With little red bands around each jar, and her firm, crabbed handwriting telling what was inside.

"In all respects!" he said again. And reached for Sam Wilkes' pudgy paw. "Congratulations, Sir! You've earned possession of the planetoid Eros. Your power-plant is among the finest it has ever been my pleasure to view; you have undeniably cleared and planted the required number of acres, your food supply is well above the minimum requirements—"

"But see here!" Wade's face was an ugly red. "I'm not satisfied, Colonel. There's something fishy about this. The farmlands we inspected were barely out of the seed stage. The corn was only knee high, the vegetables mere sprouts. These people couldn't have raised all this produce—"

Sam Wilkes spluttered helplessly, "Why I—I—"

And Pop came to his rescue. Smoothly. Suavely.

"But he did, Mr. Wade. On the farmlands across the river. Those are the early crops; the ones you've just seen are the late harvest."

"But—but you claimed those were *your* crops!"

"Did I?" Pop stroked his chin thoughtfully. "Well, maybe I was bragging a little. You see, I've been working for Mr. Wilkes. A sort of share-cropper, you might say."

"Now I get it!" howled the angry scout. "I thought so. It's skull-duggery, that's what it is! Don't you see, Colonel? These men are conspiring to defraud us. To cheat the Corporation. Moseley had deliberately given his crops and food-supply to Wilkes—"

There was again a twinkle in the Colonel's eye. He said, soberly, "And suppose you're right, Wade? What then? There's no law against a man giving away his possessions to another man, is there?

"As an inspector for the Solar Space Patrol, my only interest is in seeing that a settler's domain fulfills the requirements of the Squatter's Rights Code. Mr. Wilkes has fulfilled those requirements. I am not interested in the how or why. Therefore, under the power invested in me by the Triune Planetary Government, I hereby decide and award—"

And then a crafty brilliance illumined Wade's eyes.

"Stop!" he cried.

Colonel Travers hesitated. "Pardon, Mr. Wade?"

"Since you are such a stickler for duty, Colonel, I wish to call to your attention a further stipulation of the Squatter's Rights Code. One you have evidently forgotten. The Code says, Section 115B, Paragraph iii, 'Such requirements having been fulfilled, it shall be lawful to award the settled property to any family group comprised of at least six adults who pledge intention to make the property their permanent home—'"

Sam Wilkes said, "Well, what's the matter. Don't we intend to make Eros our permanent home?"

"I have no doubt of it, Mr. Wilkes. But I regret to inform you that you will not be able to do so, since you do not fulfill this last-mentioned paragraph."

"There's six of us!" defended Wilkes stoutly.

"But the law," insisted Wade, "requires six *adults*! May I ask,

Mr. Wilkes, how many of your family are more than twenty-one years of age!"

Dick whistled softly. Pop's jaw dropped. Wilkes' face turned crimson. And Bobby computed hastily. This was the final, devastating blow. The Wilkes household contained only four adults; Old Man Wilkes, Sam and his wife, and Red. Junior and Ginger were just kids.

With sudden regret, Bobby realized that they should have arranged their conspiracy in reverse. There were six adults in the Moseley clan, Moira having just celebrated her twenty-first birthday. But it was too late for that now. As friendly as Colonel Travers was, he could not openly countenance a flagrant, deliberate transference of all property to the Moseleys.

So their last, desperate ruse had failed. And now none of them would win ownership of Eros. All their lovely hopes and dreams had been in vain; their new-found friendship with the Wilkes a dying gesture....

Wade could not restrain himself from elaborating on the situation.

"So, my friends," he chuckled, "your deceit wins its proper reward. Under the circumstances, I shall not do what I had earlier planned on doing. I was going to give each of you, with the Corporation's compliments, a fitting reward for having so diligently opened up this new colony. Now I see no reason for so doing.

"In the future, it might be well to remember the law provides many loopholes to the ingenious man. That is a hard lesson, but a fair one. Were you but six adults—"

And then there was a sudden stir at the doorway. A deep, rumbling, familiar voice. That of Red Wilkes.

"You crow mighty loud for a bantam rooster, Mister!" he said. "But you're crowing at a false dawn. Because it so happens that we are six adults. As a matter of fact, we're more than six adults. There are *ten* of us!"

Wade spun, shocked. The others looked, too, and in all eyes there was surprise. All, that is, but Ginger. She was hugging her knees, rocking back and forth comfortably, looking very much pleased with herself and with the world in general. She said, "I knew it. I knew it all the time."

"Knew what?" said Bobby, but his question was lost in Wade's irate demand.

"Ten of you? What are you talking about? Who is this young whipper-snapper?"

"That," said Sam Wilkes conversationally, "is my son. And I'd be careful if I was you, Mister. The last guy who called him names is still pickin' up teeth. Son, I reckon you know what the hell you're talkin' about. But the rest of us don't. So if you'd please explain—?"

Red Wilkes grinned. He said, "Moira, honey." And Moira entered from the porch. There was a smile on her face and somehow there was a smile in her eyes, too, and Bobby got the strange feeling that if you could see inside her, there'd be a smile in her heart. She looked at Mom, and Mom gave a little gasp, like she could tell just by looking at Moira what Moira meant. Red Wilkes continued to grin. He said, "Colonel, commanders of space vessels have the privilege of marrying folks, haven't they?"

"Why—why, yes," said Travers.

"Then," said Red mildly, "how'd you like to get out the little black book and start tying knots? Because, you see, Moira has told me she's willing to take a chance."

Pop said, "Moira, darling, you're not just doing this because ... because...."

"No, Pop. I'm doing it because I want to. Because I love Red and he loves me. It's been that way since the day we met. We—we've been meeting secretly for the past six weeks. We meant to break the news sooner or later. And now seems to be about the best time."

"Particularly," pointed out the groom-to-be, "since our marriage turns two families into *one* family. And I think that will spike your guns, Mr. Wade?"

Wade was no longer crimson. He was purple. "You can't do this, Colonel!" he screamed. "It's illegal. Anyway, they won't be truly related. The two families will just be in-laws—"

But there was an open, admiring grin on the lips of Lieutenant-Colonel Travers, S.S.P. He said, "Maybe I *can't* do it, Mr. Wade— but by the Pleiades, I'm going to! And as for the law—according to all decisions I've ever read, in-laws are valid relatives. You're the one who was yelping about the law providing many loopholes for ingenious men. Well, here's a big, juicy loophole. How do you like it?"

Wade, howled, "I protest! It's unfair! I refuse to allow—"

Red Wilkes looked at his father hopefully. "Shall I, Pop?" he asked.

And Sam Wilkes shook his head. "No, son. It ain't fittin'. Not on your wedding day."

Which gave Dick an idea. He rose, grimly.

"It's not *my* wedding day!" he said. "Wade—"

But somehow Mr. Wade had vanished. Toward the ship.

Afterward, Colonel Travers lingered to shake hands all around.

"I commend you both," he said, "for the fine spirit you have shown; the fine work you've done in making Eros a member of the Solar family. You prove what I have always claimed—that the pioneer spirit in Man is not dead, nor will it ever die so long as there remain new frontiers to conquer.

"Well, I must go now. But I'll stop back by here on my next swing around the Belt. Perhaps a year from now, perhaps a little less. I'll bring the things you ask for. A new motor, some cloth, silverware—I have your list."

"Don't forget the books," said Pop.

"I won't." The Captain made a note.

"And the seeds." That was Old Man Wilkes.

"No. I'll bring them."

"And bring," said Moira, "a teething ring."

Eleanor said, "Oh, nonsense, Moira! In another year The Pooch will be too old for teething rings."

"Bring," said Moira doggedly, "a teething ring." And blushed.

Bobby blushed, too. It was, he thought, indecent of Moira to be so brazen. And her only married! Golly, did she have to look so far ahead? And, anyway, with Ginger standing right there....

He said, "Hey, Stinky, how about a game of quoits?"

"Suits," said Junior.

And Ginger said, "Me, too." She put her hand in Bobby's. She said, with alarming frankness, "I like you! Maybe I'll let you be my beau."

Bobby shook loose. He said, "Aw, you darn girls—"

But she had her way. She played quoits with him and Junior.

And she won. Which may have been symbolic, though it didn't occur to Bobby that way. Maybe she would always have her way. And maybe she would always win—whatever she wanted.

Yet for a while there would be peace on Eros....